# The DRIP IN the SINK

By Elizabeth Scully

## CHAPTER 1

Drip. Drip.

The sink has a big drip.

Mom must fix it. Glen can help.

Glen can get Mom's tool box.

Glen can get his tool belt.

Glen can clip his belt on.

Mom can dig in the bin and get a new part.

It is a ring.

Mom and Glen squint at the sink.

Mom and Glen hear the drip, drip.

Mom can twist the cap.

Mom can twist it left.

Mom can lift the old ring. It is junk.

Glen can set the new ring in.

Glen can help Mom twist the cap on.

Glen and Mom grin big.

The sink is fixed!

DRIP! DRIP!

The tub has a big drip.

Mom and Glen can fix the drip!

# WORD LIST

## sight words

| | | |
|---|---|---|
| a | new | the |
| fixed | old | The |
| hear | part | tool |

## consonant blends

| **initial blends** | **final blends** |
|---|---|
| clip | and |
| Drip | belt |
| drip | help |
| DRIP | junk |
| Glen | left |
| grin | lift |
| squint | must |
| twist | ring |
| | sink |
| | squint |
| | twist |

# 120 WORDS

Drip. Drip.
The sink has a big drip.
Mom must fix it. Glen can help.
Glen can get Mom's tool box.
Glen can get his tool belt.
Glen can clip his belt on.
Mom can dig in the bin and get a new part.
It is a ring.

Mom and Glen squint at the sink.
Mom and Glen hear the drip, drip.
Mom can twist the cap.
Mom can twist it left.
Mom can lift the old ring. It is junk.
Glen can set the new ring in.
Glen can help Mom twist the cap on.
Glen and Mom grin big.
The sink is fixed!
DRIP! DRIP!
The tub has a big drip.
Mom and Glen can fix the drip!

# CHERRY BLOSSOM PRESS

Published in the United States of America by Cherry Lake Publishing Group
Ann Arbor, Michigan
www.cherrylakepublishing.com

Illustrated by Laura Gomez
Book Designer: Melinda Millward

Graphic Element Credits: Cover, multiple interior pages: © memej/Shutterstock, © Eka Panova/Shutterstock, © Pand P Studio/Shutterstock, © PRebellion Works/Shutterstock

**Cherry Blossom Press** is an imprint of Cherry Lake Publishing Group.

Library of Congress Cataloging-in-Publication Data

Names: Scully, Elizabeth (Children's author), author. | Gomez, Laura, 1984- illustrator.
Title: The drip in the sink / written by Elizabeth Scully ; [illustrated by Laura Gomez].
Description: Ann Arbor, Michigan : Cherry Blossom Press, 2024. | Series: In bloom | Focuses on consonant blends. | Audience: Grades 2-3 | Summary: "Glen and Mom get to work fixing a leaky sink. Find out more in this hi-lo decodable chapter book for early readers. This book uses sequenced phonics skills and sight words to help developing readers. Original illustrations guide readers through the story"-- Provided by publisher.
Identifiers: LCCN 2023035623 | ISBN 9781668937495 (paperback) | ISBN 9781668938690 (hardcover) | ISBN 9781668939871 (ebook) | ISBN 9781668941225 (pdf)
Subjects: LCSH: Readers (Primary) | English language--Consonants--Juvenile literature. | Reading--Phonetic method--Juvenile literature. | LCGFT: Readers (Publications).
Classification: LCC PE1119.2 .S3975 2024 | DDC 428.6/2--dc23/eng/20230821
LC record available at https://lccn.loc.gov/2023035623

Cherry Lake Publishing Group would like to acknowledge the work of the Partnership for 21st Century Learning, a Network of Battelle for Kids. Please visit Battelle for Kids online for more information.

Printed in the United States of America

**Elizabeth Scully** is a classroom teacher and reading specialist for 20 years in Western New York. A graduate of Cornell University, she continued her studies in Language and Literacy at Harvard University. She is a trained Reading Recovery teacher and certified at the Associate Level with the Orton-Gillingham Academy. When she is not crafting stories about the animals in her life, Elizabeth is busy trundling her family of boys around town.

Note from publisher: Websites change regularly, and their future contents are outside of our control. Supervise children when conducting any recommended online searches for extended learning opportunities.